Fletcher

The Faithful Potato

A Story of Faith for All Ages

Bob White

To order additional copies of this book, contact:
Xlibris
844-714-8691
www.Xlibris.com
Orders@Xlibris.com

ISBN: Softcover   978-1-6698-0370-6
        EBook   978-1-6698-0369-0

Print information available on the last page

Rev. date: 12/13/2021

Dedicated to the memory of my son, Bryan Fletcher White who taught me about Faith and even now from Heaven is still spreading sunshine to all the people he knew.

Fletcher

Potatoes

Russet
.89 Lb

PURPLE
2.29 Lb

REDSKIN
1.89 Lb

YAMS
2.09 Lb

YUKON GOL
1.99 Ll

An innocent redskin lying on a shelf

Awaiting my sale, exploring myself

Thrown into a bag with lots o' more spuds

Some of 'em strangers, some of em' buds

Thru the express lane and into a car

To a cook in a kitchen,
cause that's who we are.

Why it seems so quick,
being washed in a strainer

Not got long, why that's a no-brainer

Just as we're dumped
and meeting the chopper,

Cook drops two taters, me and a whopper

Picks up the big guy, leaves me for the sweeper

Why even for food, I don't seem a keeper.

In the dark, on the floor, in like a cove,

created by a gap between a
counter and the stove.

Along comes a broom
and big industrial dust pan,

Into where I am swept by a giant of a man.

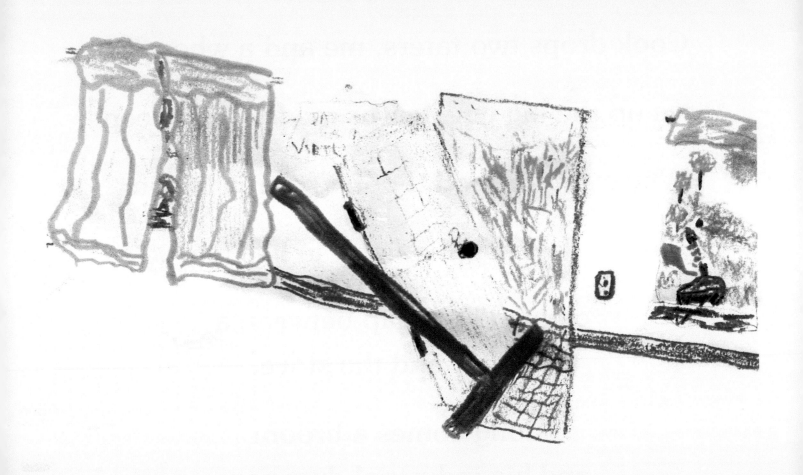

Carried out back, in this pan,
with these sweepings

If I wasn't a potato I'd surely be weeping

Big man sets broom down by the door post

and tosses us sweepings to lie near the compost.

why a potato all alone just me on the ground

so I tater up and survey, by looking around

because I am cozy, means I love my new soil

and to think I could be coming to boil.

The sun is a beauty, there's plenty to drink

Why perfect for growing potatoes I think

My eyes have been opened,
I've started to sprout

and my baby redskins are rooting about

Why the months have been awesome,
since I opened my eyes,

And Hey! I'm just a potato you guys

Because my eyes looked up,
why they saw the light

And redskin potatoes are everywhere in sight.

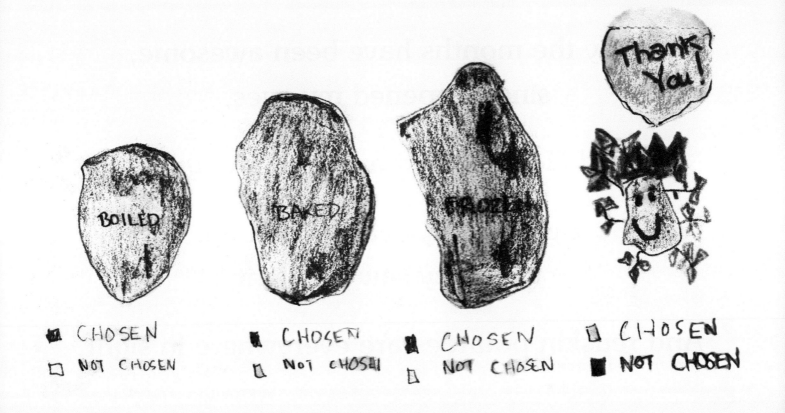

BOILED
■ CHOSEN
☐ NOT CHOSEN

BAKED
■ CHOSEN
☐ NOT CHOSEN

FROZEN
■ CHOSEN
☐ NOT CHOSEN

Thank You!
☐ CHOSEN
■ NOT CHOSEN

Sold to be dinner, born to be a stud

I thank God, why I'm a heck of a spud

I'm thankful I fell so not to be chosen

Why I could have wound up either
boiled, baked or frozen.

Printed in the United States
by Baker & Taylor Publisher Services